How Baseball Began
by Paul M. Kramer

How Baseball Began by Paul M. Kramer

© Paul M. Kramer August 2010. All Rights Reserved.

Aloha Publishers LLC
333 Dairy Road, Suite 106
Kahului, HI 96732
www.alohapublishers.com

Inquiries, comments or further information are available at, www. alohapublishers.com.

Illustrations by Catanzariti Studios, acatanz@gmail.com.

ISBN 13 (EAN): 978-0-9819745-9-0   Printed in China
Library of Congress Control Number (LCCN): 2009944047

How Baseball Began
by Paul M. Kramer

Aloha
PUBLISHERS
Books & Stories by Paul M. Kramer

Once upon a time, long, long ago,
in a place where just about anything would grow,
where the temperature could rise to over 100 degrees,
where often there was none or very little breeze,
lived a boy named Clem who pruned trees.

There was a beautiful long straight branch of wood,
that did not grow in the direction that it should.
So Clem cut that branch off down by its base.
Shortly thereafter another tree would grow in that space.
Clem took that branch of wood and stored it in a safe and dry place.

It was getting late and was time to return
to the farm.
The sun had just set and the sky was
unusually calm.
After dinner Clem sat on the porch with his
little brother Ed.
Clem had a book and to his little brother
he read.
Less than an hour later Clem and Ed were
ready for bed.

Clem was cleaning up some nuts that had fallen to the ground.
They had rolled down the hill and formed a large mound.
Clem took out his new wood branch thinking he could have some fun.
He threw each nut high into the air one by one.
Then he swung the wood branch and hit every nut until there was none.

He told his best friend Fred about his day and what he had done.
Fred said, "If I bring my own wood branch, could I join in on the fun?"
There were only a couple of nuts on the ground that could be found.
But there were plenty of peaches they could hit that were small and round.
After playing for hours they stopped after a peach hit Clem's basset hound.

For Clem's birthday he got a special gift that was called a ball.
It was made from rubber and it could be thrown against a wall.
You could bounce it and the best part is it would come back to you.
There were so many other fun things that this ball could do.
Clem and Fred tied a hoop to a tree and practiced
throwing the ball through.

Carl, another friend of Clem's, showed up at Clem's house one day.
Seeing Clem and Fred playing and laughing, Carl said, "Can I play?"
They came up with an idea that would be good for them all.
One would catch, one would throw, and the other would hit the ball.
They took turns and rotated the rest of the day until it was nightfall.

They had so much fun they decided to play at least once a week.
Occasionally one of the boys would hit the ball into the creek.
"If only we had more players to catch the ball after it was hit," Clem said.
Clem, Carl and Ed talked to other boys and before long news had spread.
There were so many kids who wanted to play, according to Fred.

They all agreed to meet in the large empty field on Saturday.
The kids who were there were really excited to play.
The large field looked like a diamond shaped square.
Any ball hit to the left, the right or the rear of the square was foul,
all else was fair.
They split into two teams, one batting, and the other catching
and spread out their players everywhere.

After a batter hit the ball, that batter would then run to the first base.
White wood square bases called 1st, 2nd, 3rd, and home were at specific places.
Each boy practiced both hitting and fielding that day.
They were truly happy they were given a chance to play.
When asked how about the same time next week, every boy said okay.

The following Saturday some of the boys brought thicker branches.
The thicker branches improved their chances of hitting the ball giving them
an added advantage.
They whittled and shaped the branch to get a better grip and called it a bat.
It wasn't too long or too short, it wasn't too thin or too fat.
The only boy who preferred a longer thinner branch was a boy named Matt.

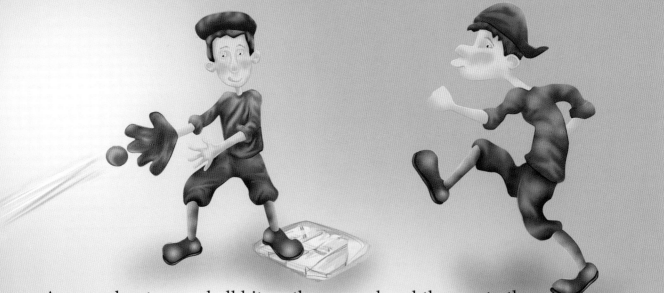

A ground out was a ball hit on the ground and thrown to the first baseman before the hitter ran there.

A fly out was a ball hit and caught by the fielding team while the ball was still in the air.

When a batter swings and misses three times, that was called a strikeout.

The local saddle maker made padded gloves from leather scraps to protect the fielder's hands, which were also called mitts.

When someone reached the first base after hitting a ball that no one caught, that was called a hit.

Complete innings were when both teams had taken their turn at bat.

Each team was allowed three outs in an inning and no more than that.

Any player on the hitting team, who reached home base safely, scored a run.

After the completion of nine innings if the score wasn't tied the game was done.

The team who has scored the most runs at the end of the game had won.

News spread quickly about this new terrific game of bat and ball.
Kids getting together and playing outdoors was certainly fun for all.
Friends and relatives came to the fields to watch the players play.
The entire game sometimes took more than three hours of the day.
Attending this game was the Mayor of the town, Danny O'Shay.

Clem and his friends really loved playing this new great game.
They called it playing bat and ball and to them, that was its name.
They never dreamed its popularity would grow and grow and grow.
Those original boys had no clue, for how could they possibly know.
This great game of baseball would be America's favorite sport of tomorrow.

As the game grew in popularity, it was officially named baseball.

It was one sport where it did not matter too much if you were short or tall.

It was a sport where skills and abilities were truly unlimited.

So that is how baseball began according to Clem, Carl and Fred.

Do you think it was a rumor or did it begin the way those boys said?

Baseball

Can be enjoyed by the entire family,
played with a bat, a ball and a glove.
said to be America's favorite past time,
a game that most everybody has grown to love.

Requires discipline, skill and teamwork,
the team who scores the most runs is the team that has won.
Players from little league to college and beyond,
benefit from the exercise or just having fun in the sun.

Baseball is seen by millions in person and on TV,
enthusiastically awaiting the start and finish of this amazing game.
Experience and ability vary greatly from player to player.
Baseball greats are compensated with fortune and fame.

Paul M Kramer

Just Published by Paul M. Kramer

Bullies Beware! – Mikey didn't want to be bullied anymore. He was also afraid and embarrassed to tell anyone about being bullied. Bullying has escalated in recent years and has become a very serious problem that must be dealt with. It takes a lot of courage to stand up to a bully and Mikey finally did. This informative book is a must-read for the parents of young kids who either may, or are having problems with bullies.

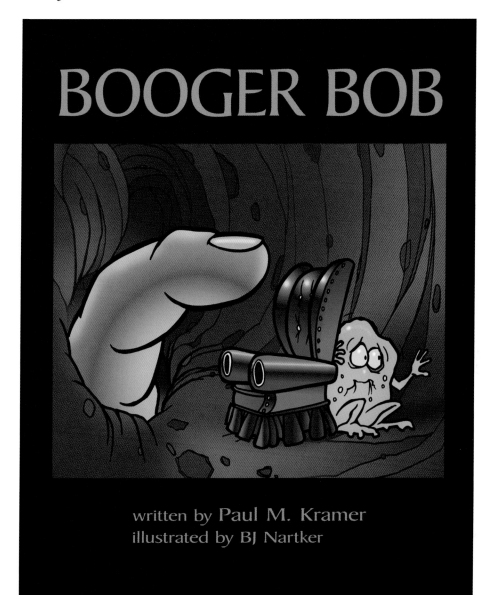

BOOGER BOB

written by Paul M. Kramer
illustrated by BJ Nartker

Booger Bob – It is difficult to teach children proper personal hygiene. This cute story is a funny representation of what people do with what comes out of their noses and how they dispose of it. Although the subject matter could be considered gross by many, there is a lesson to be learned after the laughter stops.

About the Author

Paul M Kramer lives in Hawaii on the Island of Maui, but was born and raised in New York City. He moved to the Rainbow and Aloha State of Hawaii in 1995 with his wife Cindy and their then infant son, Lukas. After being in Hawaii for about nine years, Mr. Kramer's true passion in life was awakened. He began writing children's books that deal with important issues that kids face today. Mr. Kramer's books are written in rhyme, are easy to read and make learning fun.